HOTEL GAMES

A Sexy Snowed-in Holiday Novella

CAT WYNN

Stay cozy,
stay smutty.

Happy
Holidays
— Cat Wynn

Stay Cozy,

Stay Smithy.

Hopeful
Holidays!

— Okayla

Hotel Games

Cover Design By: Cover Apothecary at coverapothecary.com
Editor: Brittni Van at Overbooked Author Services

To you and to Elfie, a very good friend

Chapter 1

OLIVIA COUPER SUCKED ON THE MINTY LOOP OF A MINIATURE candy cane. She'd found it attached to a small, neatly wrapped Christmas present sitting on the passenger seat of Henry Pointe's old Nissan Sentra.

"From a patient..." Henry had murmured when Olivia snatched up the candy. She tossed the small but hefty box in the back and tucked the extra candy cane in the cup holder.

As a thirty-three year old cardiothoracic surgical resident, Henry's car was absolute trash. But Olivia wasn't trying to complain, at least he had candy.

She also wouldn't have minded so much being in his old rusted-out vehicle if he hadn't insisted on driving it in the middle of a snow storm instead of taking her very-nice-mind-you-not-even-a-year-old-yet Range Rover instead. Which would have withstood the harsh North Carolina blizzard just fine under pressure, ensuring that they made it to their Friendsmas mountain house in Asheville.

But *noooo*. Henry had to have his way.

And okay, so it was kind of her fault too. She'd been running late with a client who'd wanted to micromanage every hair follicle on his head. And Henry and Olivia weren't supposed to even be traveling together, as Olivia had many times over learned her lessons about occupying too much personal space with Henry...

But the temptation of convenience was too great. They lived in the same building, it just made sense, for the sake of saving time to reach out to Henry when Olivia couldn't get out of her appointment. She'd texted him with good will, and it was nice that he agreed to help her. He even agreed to gather her bags and picked her up curbside. Plus, she wouldn't get so bored in the car all by herself during the journey from Charleston to Asheville.

Sometimes Olivia and Henry could be friendly like that.

But sometimes he was annoying. Like right now.

"Just pull over here..." she pointed to the exit off the highway. "You're making me nervous."

"Don't back seat drive," Henry grumbled, but he was struggling to steady the wheel as his car hobbled through the snow, his already brooding face looking even more serious than usual.

Despite her annoyance, she let her gaze slip down his body as she crunched the rest of the candy cane. He was tall and a little lean, but also cut. Like the kind of guy who was just born with a six pack. Which he did faintly have, probably from all the long distance running he did early in the morning. Olivia would eye it up whenever he'd stretch his arms, propelling his shirt the tiniest bit above his waist band, revealing the line of dark hair trailing from his belly button.

Olivia on the other hand never cared for working out and her soft body showed it. Although, she was pretty sure she was destined to be soft no matter what. She loved the rounded curves of her frame. In high school when the social rules felt strict and stifling, she thought she had to be skinny and tiny and basically disappear into nothingness to feel good about herself. But once she hit college, she decided *fuck it*. She'd rather eat and sleep and live how she wanted, feeling completely whole.

As a hairstylist, she loved to create visually pleasing aesthetics. In her humble opinion, her body was one of those visually pleasing aesthetics, and she treated it just so. Currently her long, platinum bob was streaked with a bright pink fringe.

Olivia's stomach lurched as Henry shakily turned off the highway, but luckily a Celebration Inn was right off the exit. Henry flipped on his blinker and they half coasted, half slid into the parking lot. Precipitation poured from the sky in windy, white sheets while the snow banks swelled steadily at the sides of the road. The inside of the car was almost stiflingly warm, but that was better than the bitter outside freeze.

Olivia tapped the map on her phone. "Okay, we're still ninety miles from your uncle's house. August said she got there last night. "

August was Henry's sister and one of Olivia's best friends. She was the one who had planned their Friendsmas trip to Asheville. "This doesn't look good. I'm gonna call her."

At the exact moment August picked up the call, a huge pile of snow dropped from a tree branch directly onto the front windshield, startling the shit out of Olivia.

Her words came out frantically. "Holy fucking shit, August you won't fucking believe what it looks like out here." She craned her neck to see out of the small uncovered section of the window. Car after car pulled over to the side of the road. "We're pretty much stranded."

"We're not stranded yet, we're in a Celebration Inn parking lot," said Henry.

"Who's that? Is that Henry?" August's voice came from the other end of the line. "I thought you were driving yourself after your last client."

August wasn't a fan of last minute plan changes, and

Olivia might've had a bad habit of changing plans whenever it suited her. *Oops.* "Girl, I was, but that bastard kept me forty five minutes late, and I didn't have time to run home to get any of my things. Henry picked them up for me so I hitched a ride with him. Easy peasy." *See, a perfectly reasonable explanation.*

But then August didn't sound so happy. "So, Henry's spending Christmas with us?"

"Duh. He's your brother. Wait, Henry wasn't invited?" *Oops again!* Olivia had assumed because they were using August and Henry's uncle's house for their holiday that it wouldn't be a big deal for Henry to come either. In her own family, people just showed up whenever they felt like it. But apparently that was weird. In the periphery of her vision, red and blue lights flashed from the side of the road. "Oh! Oh! The cops just rolled up. Shit *Shit.*"

"Don't tell me." But it sounded like August already knew what was happening.

Two cops got out of their car, blocking the road beside them. "They're shutting down the roads."

"You're kidding."

Olivia sighed. "At least we're already at a hotel. See! Safety first!"

"Olivia. I'm here *alone* with your friend Jack, who is a complete and total stranger to me. You can't leave me with this himbo!"

Olivia almost clapped her hands together in excitement. "Oh, Jack made it already? That's so exciting! Himbo, yes. That's a good word for him." Very astute observation.

"Who's Jack?" Henry asked. Olivia waved him off.

Olivia had invited her old friend Jack to stay with the crew for Christmas. Years ago, Jack used to bartend with her in Charleston, but he moved and now worked as a chef at a hip downtown restaurant.

She cupped the phone to her mouth and turned her face

to the window. "Isn't he so unbelievably hot? Super nice too. I'm so happy he made it."

Olivia had an inkling Jack and August might hit it off, and when he told her he didn't have plans for the holiday, she couldn't resist inviting him along.

"Who *is* Jack?" Henry tapped her arm, but again she shrugged him off. "Shut. Up," she mouthed silently.

"Well, I'm *not* so happy he made it," August hissed. "You know I'm not good with small talk. Or strangers! Fuck. *Fuck.* This trip was supposed to be about the three of us, You, me, and Elliot. It was supposed to be absolutely perfect. And now Henry. And this snowstorm. And...*Jack.* Elliot better get here, stat."

Elliot Sheer was the third member of their girl group, and by far the craftiest of the three. She worked as a traveling photographer and lived everyday like it was her last—for better or for worse.

But Olivia felt terrible because August was right, this was a big Christmas for the three women, and her attention was divided. Cars with emergency lights were stranded on the side of the road, and the parking lot was full. She looked over to Henry. "Should we be worried? Parking lot's chaos...I forgot to pack my mittens."

"What'd you say?" asked August.

But a bleak realization slowly descended upon Olivia. "It's not looking good, August. I don't think we're gonna make it tonight."

"You can't leave me here with that man." The creep of desperation tinged August's voice. "He brought a wild animal into the house."

Olivia's ears perked up. "Exsqueeze me? Like what? A rat? A racoon?"

"No...he brought a...he brought a *kitten*," she whispered.

Olivia tried not to laugh. August could be a stickler and

slow to warm up. But kittens were so cute! "Oh no, the handsome chef brought a kitten to the holiday mountain house."

August sighed. "Can you try to have a little sympathy? I'm not like you. This is really uncomfortable for me."

Sometimes August just needed some gentle coaching when it came to making new friends. Olivia softened her voice. "Sweetie, sweetie, sweetie. I know it's not ideal, and I want to be there just as much as you. Do you think I'm happy about missing our first get together in three years? I'm just trying to keep up a good attitude. And look, I'm not god, I can't account for Mother Nature. If we try to drive ninety miles in this weather, we're probably gonna die. Do you want that blood on your hands? Or would you rather hang out with a handsome dude and a kitten for a while by yourself? Might I remind you, your guilt is even stronger than your awkwardness. Just have him feed you, he's an amazing chef."

August sighed. "You're right. I just want everyone to be safe. I'll text Elliot. Elliot can make her way through anything. Right?"

"I'm sure you're right." But judging by the weather, Olivia wasn't so sure. People started to swarm the entrance of the hotel. At the sight, Olivia's panic spiked.

If everyone was trying to get a room, that would mean the hotel would run out of rooms. And if that happened... "Gotta call you back. Everyone's making a mad rush for the Celebration Inn now. Shit! Henry, get out and run in front of that crowd! Can you get me a room with a view of the pool?"

For once, Henry didn't make her life difficult. "Goddammit..." he muttered under his breath, but he snapped open his seatbelt and stumbled out of the car. She barely heard August's voice on the other end before hanging up. "Okay, text me in the morning!"

She fumbled with her seatbelt, opening the door to chase after Henry, and shivered when she was met with the cold, wet, bitter wind.

OLIVIA TAPPED HER FOOT, arms crossed, waiting in the line at the front desk. When the dawdling couple ahead finally turned and headed toward the elevator, Olivia marched over, Henry behind her.

"Hello, ma'am," the receptionist greeted them with a slow, deadpan drawl.

"Hey. Hello. Yes, we'd like two rooms, thank you. King bed, highest floor available, no smoking obviously. And can I have one with a view of the pool? I know it's weird, but I have a thing about always having to be around water because I'm a triple water sign."

"God, you're such a princess," Henry gruffed.

"Thank youuuu." Olivia gave Henry a sneering smile which he returned in kind. Except when he did it, it was kind of sexy, which annoyed her even more.

"Yes, I'll get on that right away." The receptionist mimed typing over his keyboard. Then he pushed up his glasses and cleared his throat. "I have one room with a queen bed. Second floor. It overlooks the parking lot."

"Well, shit." She scratched her head. "What do we do?"

Henry leaned over the counter. "Listen, I know you don't know this about me, but I save lives. I'm a surgeon—"

Olivia cut him off. "Nope, nope, nope. Gonna stop you there. Bad strategy." She clasped her hands together, placing them on the counter. "We're willing to work with you. What can we do to get another room?" She reached into her handbag and flashed a one hundred dollar bill.

The receptionist unblinkingly stared at her. "Perhaps you could import some raw materials and build one yourself. Please step aside."

She and Henry exchanged a look which Olivia interpreted as: *We're gonna be in deep shit if we don't take this room.*

She smoothed her hair at the side of her head. "Fine. We'll take the room. Overlooking the… parking lot."

"Superb." The receptionist slid the plastic key over the counter. "Elevator is to your left. Continental breakfast is served from six to nine am." Then he tilted his head to see past Olivia's shoulder. "Sorry, folks, we're out of vacancies. Please try La Quinta Inn next door or the motel across the street where all the murders happened. Merry Christmas."

Behind them people moaned, zipping up their coats and slipping on their hats.

"I guess we should be grateful we got a room at all." Olivia sighed.

"Speak for yourself. This is what I get for doing you a favor."

"Well, no one said you had to join us for the holidays," Olivia huffed even though she quite literally had invited him. She hiked her designer weekender bag over her shoulder. Henry had his old camping backpack strapped on, which looked like it'd already been through a blizzard or two. Still, Henry was fastidious and clean, something Olivia liked. Not that she'd ever tell him.

They approached the silver doors of the elevator, their reflections distorted and drawn out staring back at them. Henry pushed the button. *Ding.*

And like Christmas lights illuminating on a timer, reality hit Olivia: she was going to spend the night with Henry Pointe. *Oh fuck.*

Chapter 2

"SO THIS IS WHAT TWO HUNDRED BUCKS A NIGHT GETS YOU IN the middle of a snowstorm, huh?" Henry shrugged out of his backpack and set it next to the door.

"Awww, don't worry, baby. I'll cover the cost. I was born to be a sugar momma." Olivia surveyed the small hotel room. It was standard chain-hotel fair as far as anyone was concerned. The queen-sized bed was square in the middle of the room, the duvet pulled tight across the mattress with crisp corners as hotels often had.

The walls were blank except for three corporatized photographs, above the bed, of mallards taking flight. So much for Christmas spirit.

"Well, this is fucking festive." She unzipped her long turquoise winter coat, shrugged it off her shoulders and hung it up in the closet.

She should be with her best college friends, whom she hadn't even seen in three long years, at a beautiful house with an Appalchian view. Instead she was here, with her frenemy, Henry. In this sterile hotel room. A prison of her own making.

She glared at him just to feel better.

"What the hell was that for?" He said furrowing his brows.

But she didn't answer, instead she tossed her bag onto the bed and unzipped it, yanking out an oversized sweatshirt and pulling it on over her t-shirt. Even though the heat pumped through the air vents, the winter chill crept in.

"Where will you sleep?" she asked as she poked her head through the hole of the sweatshirt, pulling her hair from her nape.

"I'm sleeping on the bed. Where will _you_ sleep?"

"That's a funny joke."

"God, you're such a goddamn princess."

"Exactly. So, we agree then. Me, on the bed."

For a moment, Olivia could've sworn she saw something dark glimmer over Henry's eyes, but then he scoffed as usual. "I'm not arguing with you. You can either sleep on the bed with me or you can sleep on the floor by yourself. This isn't up for discussion."

She rolled her eyes. "You think you're the boss of everyone."

"I am the boss of many people actually. I just don't want to deal with your incessant whining."

"For the record, most people love my whining."

"Who do you mean by _most people?_"

She shrugged, settling at the edge of the bed, picking at her freshly manicured mountain peak nails. She'd had them half done in candy cane stripes and the other half white with sparkly silver stars. Some people might have referred to her as _extra_. But some people didn't know how to live.

"Nobody's ever complained about my _whining_ before. It's almost as if you just have a particularly grumpy disposition."

Then her eyes went wide as Henry reached behind his neck and yanked off his forest green sweater, revealing a black t-shirt underneath. He folded the sweater, unzipping his backpack, sliding it neatly back in.

"Hey! Keep your clothes on," Olivia huffed. But also, she wasn't *not* enjoying the view.

"It's stuffy as hell in here." He walked to the window, leaning forward and inspecting the glass. "Can't even open this fucking thing."

"Are you kidding? Aren't you cold?" She rubbed her upper arms, finding her fingertips a little chilled.

Henry turned around, his hands on the ledge in front of the window, his tall, lean silhouette highlighted by the light behind him. "Not even a little."

But what a surprise, as usual, they weren't on the same page. One was always hot while the other was always cold. And she never knew who would be which.

And with that answer, a chill ran right down her arms.

"I'M BORED." Olivia rested her back against the headboard, her arms crossed, her phone dangling from her hand. She couldn't keep playing mindless games on her phone. And she didn't have any more advice to dole out to August about her situation with Jack either. Although she and Elliot were having a great time razzing August about it.

Still, as it stood, August was stranded at the mountain house, Olivia was stranded at a hotel, and Elliot was stranded at an airport. Not exactly how their Friendsmas was supposed to go.

But Olivia was optimistic that Elliot could entertain herself at the airport. And August...well, she could very easily make friends with Jack.

Unlike Olivia and Henry, who were at this moment definitely *not* friends. They were in their enemy stage.

"Read a book," Henry suggested. He sat at the chair next to the window, his long legs propped up on the window ledge.

Outside, the snow spilled like a snipped bag of flour over the dark sky.

"Uh, what book? The only book here is the Bible in the bedside drawer."

"Maybe you should give it a try," he chuckled to himself.

"Whatever. You're even less fun than usual."

He bent his elbow and rubbed his shoulder, stretching his neck. "I'm under a lot of stress at work. And you know...other things."

"Other things like *Anna*..." she said the words before she could stop herself. *Oops.* Everything was a game with Henry, one where she never seemed to have the upper hand. Whenever she got it, she had to play hard in order to stay on top. Caring too much about Henry's personal life would definitely put her in the loser's column.

She prepared for a snarky comeback, but Henry stiffened up. "None of your business."

"Oh?" *Shut up, Olivia.* But curiosity killed the hair stylist.

"You care about Anna? I thought you were dating that Liam guy, or Payton or Parker or whatever the fuck his stupid name was. With all the muscles and all the..." He made an arm flexing movement. Olivia hadn't even dated Liam, the guy Henry was referring to. Liam was just a random Tinder meet up she'd met at a bar. A bar where she happened to often run into Henry.

She didn't purposely take dates to the bar she *knew* Henry frequented after long shifts. She lived just as close to that establishment as he did. She had every right to go there and coincidentally run into him from time to time.

Sometimes, when Olivia didn't have a date and Henry was in an off moment with Anna, they would even sit and get drinks together. Sometimes they even laughed.

She remembered the first time it happened. Henry had moved into her building a few months prior. She avoided him as much as she could, but it wasn't really that difficult, as they had very different schedules.

Henry worked all the time, and Olivia tried to work the least amount she possibly could. Still, her hair business was booming. She'd finally established herself as somebody.

One Saturday evening, Olivia had worked a long day and needed to blow off some steam, so she stopped by the bar. Sauntering up to a barstool with her usual bravado, wearing her usual attire of black pants and a see-through mesh top with a black bra, coupled with her floral print boots. Nothing too wild, especially not for her. But, lo and behold, as soon as she sat down, who sat down right next to her at the counter but none other than Henry Pointe.

At first, they tossed quips back and forth. But after a drink or two, they simmered their banter and got to talking. Henry was looking scruffy and tired from his long hours. Olivia offered to cut his hair.

"You've got a good head of hair," she said, offering him a rare compliment. She was actually dying to get her hands on it.

He scratched at his head. Had he blushed? "Thanks. It's not as cool as yours though."

She shrugged. "I know."

He never took her up on the offer.

But that's when she began her habit of checking in at the bar. Just in case she'd catch a glimpse of him.

Besides, they served a great Pinot Noir. God, she could really go for a drink. She was feeling antsy. And the longer she spent in the room with Henry, the more she had to *look* at him.

He was handsome.

Fuuuuuck. Don't do this Olivia. You always fucking do this when you're alone with Henry. No self control, none at all! Why are you this way?

But she could never help herself.

"Are you jealous?" she asked in a teasing, and not very nice, tone. "You sound jealous."

"Am I jealous of the fucking basement dwelling podcasters you take out every weekend." He scoffed. She watched with rapt interest as he ran his hand through his dark hair. "No, I wouldn't call that jealousy. I'd say it's somewhere closer to pity."

"How do you know it's every weekend then?" She smiled innocently. "That just proves how popular I am."

Henry didn't respond with anything more than a grunt which disappointed her a bit. She was goading him, wasn't she? For a reaction.

Every time she had *an incident* with Henry, she deeply regretted it the next day, never knowing where they stood afterwards. He was so gruff and grim and distant. Kind of like now.

Olivia wanted to perspire beneath the hot flames of love. What Henry was giving her was so far away from that, he might as well have been the winter blizzard himself. Fucking grinch.

Her stomach grumbled. "I'm hungry."

"Best I got is a bottle of wine in the car. But it's supposed to be a gift for August."

"That's thoughtful, I guess." She let her head fall back on the headboard. "Ugh, what I wouldn't give to make it to the house. Jack is a chef. A chef! I bet August is eating like a goddamn queen."

"Jack, huh?" Henry didn't look up from his tablet as he said it, but this time Olivia could just sense his jealousy.

"Yeah, Jack. You know the guy with over two hundred thousand TikTok followers? Women love to watch him bake sexy desserts."

Henry scratched his head. "You can't bake a sexy dessert, that doesn't even make sense." He sounded skeptical but also nervous. *Ah ha!* She liked that.

"Jack can."

"So you're into him. Of course you are." He shook his head as if to say *I knew you would be.*

She wasn't. "Maybe." In fact, she really only invited Jack because he had no one to spend the holidays with, and because she knew he'd hit it off with August. *And August could use a good fuck, that was for sure.* "All I care about now is how goddamn hungry I am."

Her stomach gurgled again, and she put her hands on her belly.

Abruptly, Henry stood, a frown etched into his angular face.

"Where're you going?" Olivia asked as he stomped from the window over to the door. But he didn't answer her, and the door closed with a snick.

"*Jesus...*" she murmured to herself, rolling to her side to look at her phone. She had a message from Elliot Sheer, her beautiful best friend.

Elliot: You fuck Henry yet?

Unlike August, Elliot was deeply aware of Olivia and Henry's *sordid* history. She'd tried to disclose even the vaguest of implications to August before but August just shoved her fingers in her ears and said "La la la la la, I don't want to know whatever it is that goes on between you and my brother... la la la la la." So, Elliot was the only one she could really confide in.

Olivia: Henry and I don't fuck. We hang out, we fight, and we occasionally hook up at inopportune moments and then pretend like it never happened later.

Elliot: Sounds hot.

Olivia: Sometimes we're even friendly with each other.

Elliot: Sounds less hot.

Elliot: Do you think this guy looks like a Taurus?

The picture that followed was nothing more than the back of a man's head.

He was tall with broad shoulders, neatly trimmed ash brown hair and a grey henley. Elliot was waiting in line at the airline's gate at the airport.

Olivia: I think he looks like one of your targets.

Elliot: Target! What do you mean by that?

Olivia: Just that you love to make desperate men fall in love with you.

Elliot: You know me well. So, Virgo then?

Olivia: Sure, let's go with Virgo.

Elliot: Don't forget to wear protection tonight! Kisses!

Olivia shook her head. Elliot was ridiculous. Protection? She was on birth control.

The door opened abruptly again, Henry's long frame stepped into the room and his arms were filled.

"What in the hell is all that?"

He approached the bed and then let his arms open, dropping a heap of packaged snacks to the mattress in a shiny pile. "You're hungry." He gestured toward the snacks on the bed. "They're not sexy desserts, but they're all that's available."

"Where'd you even get all this?"

"Vending machine on the fifth floor."

"Did you buy out the entire thing?"

"I didn't know what you like."

"You could have just asked."

"You want it or not?"

"Yeah, of course I fucking want it." Olivia rummaged through the pile on the bed, pilfering a bag of Skittles and snapping it open. "Here, have this…" She threw a packet of salt and vinegar chips at Henry. "Since you're so fucking salty and sour all the time."

He sat at the end of the bed, bag of chips on his lap. "I actually do like these."

She watched with furtive interest as Henry fiddled with his car keys, working the jagged end into the cork of the bottle of wine he'd brought back.

"What kind of wine is that?" she asked.

"Pinot Noir."

"Hmm. My favorite kind."

Henry glanced up, his forearm muscles tensed and veins bulged down to his wrist as the cork popped out. "Yeah, I'm aware."

His answer gave her pause, and she knew it was going to be a very long night indeed.

Chapter 3

"HOW COME YOU ONLY PICKED OUT THE JUNK FOOD? OF course you don't even touch the trail mix or the dried fruit or the protein bar." Henry gestured at the many strewn about wrappers on the bed, shiny like tinsel and colorful as glass ornaments.

The two of them were splayed out side by side, legs stretched long on top of the fluffy hotel duvet. They'd managed to even be cordial while they ate.

Olivia gulped faucet water from a mug that she'd found in the coffee station next to the closet. At least they'd have shitty instant coffee in the morning. "I was starving. Been on my feet all day."

Henry gulped from his own mug, but his was filled with wine. "So have I, but I didn't eat six bags of Skittles."

"You bought them!" Then the corners of her mouth upturned in a devilish way. "Are you criticizing my body?" She knew even the suggestion would freak him out, but she wanted to see him squirm.

His eyes went big, and he swallowed hard. "It's not about your body, it's about your health."

"Please. Says the man chugging wine from a mug."

He lifted his mug. "Yeah, well. As a doctor, I don't care about my health. Cheers."

Olivia sighed. "Can't cheers with water, it's bad luck. You might as well pour me some." She downed the rest and then shoved her cup in front of his face. He gave her a sardonic look, grabbed the bottle from his nightstand and poured.

"Whoa, whoa, whoa. That's enough. Jesus, you trying to drink away your feelings or what?"

"Can't handle a big girl pour?"

She rolled her eyes. "Oh no, that's right. You don't have feelings."

"What's that supposed to mean?"

She giggled, sipping at the wine enjoying how it warmed her up right in the center of her chest. "Oh, come on."

"Come on, what?"

"You're not exactly a Waffle House when it comes to being open. You're as closed off as that window over there. Why are you looking at me like that?"

Henry's eyes had narrowed, his head tilted. "I can't believe you, *you* of all people are accusing me of being closed off. You're one of the most closed off people I've ever met. You can't even be in a relationship. I was in a relationship for four whole years —"

"—Was it four *whole* years, really?" As far as she knew, Henry and Anna were always on and off. Mostly off. But always happened to be on again at the worst times. Anna was a nice respectable attorney, slender and blonde. She hated Anna.

Henry took another sip. "It was a hell of a lot longer than you've got under your belt. And I know a thing or two about what's under your belt."

Heat burned her cheeks. They'd *never* outwardly acknowledged the times they'd hooked up. They'd just go on their merry way afterwards and act like nothing happened.

He was inching into new territory, territory that brought them scarily close to the truth about Olivia's feelings.

She decided to feign ignorance. Better that than to give him anything else to work with. His ego was big enough as it was, and she didn't need him knowing that she actually masturbated to the memory of those hookups every now and then. She tucked her hair behind her ear primly. "I don't know what you're talking about."

"Oh really? That's how you want to play it?"

Her gaze crept over to see that his head was turned to her. His eyes were such a dark brown and framed with such dark, downturned fringe that he almost looked sad sometimes.

"Play what?" She placed her mug on the nightstand and picked up her phone, opening one of the dating apps she had downloaded. Quickly, she began to swipe without thinking much about it. *Right, right, left, left, left, right.*

"What are you doing?" he asked, leaning to look over her shoulder.

"Hey!" She covered her screen.

"Oh my god, are you swiping on a dating app in the middle of a conversation with me while we're *stranded in a blizzard.* Have you no decency? And how do you expect to get to these men? Zamboni?"

"Don't underestimate men's desire to see me."

"You're being absolutely ridiculous right now. What do you even expect to accomplish from that?"

"Maybe I'm just a horny person." *Oops.* In her head, those words had sounded like a joke, but now that she'd said them out loud they most certainly did not sound funny.

He let out a big exhale, but she avoided eye contact. Why were her thigh muscles suddenly clenching? Was she a little buzzed? She'd only had a few sips.

There was a stretch of nothing between them before his voice broke the silence. "How horny, exactly?"

She squeezed her eyes shut and just-like-fucking-that a fork in the proverbial road appeared before them. It always went down like this. First, they would bicker. Then, they would hook up.

They were walking the path now, the one they'd been down several times before. She slugged back her mug of wine and turned over on her side, still swiping, aware that he could see her screen. "Not horny enough for you."

"That's what you think."

She craned her neck looking over her shoulder at him. He sat up, sliding his legs over the side of the bed.

"What do you think'll happen, Henry? You think I'll get so horny being around you that I won't be able to control myself? Newsflash. You ain't that great." Depending on what scale one might be weighing greatness on, at least.

He brushed her off. "That's how it's always happened before." Again, he was saying the quiet part out loud.

Then he stood from the bed, reached behind his neck again and yanked off his shirt, giving her glimpses of his muscled but lean back.

The shirt hit her on the head after he flung it off. "Hey!" She pulled it off her hair and the faint scent of him filled her nostrils. That familiar fucking scent.

Then he marched into the bathroom and shut the door. The sound of the spray of water from the faucet was audible.

If she wasn't horny before, well, she was now. Should she masturbate? Was she really so desperate? Normally, no, but these weren't normal circumstances. She rubbed the t-shirt against her nose trying to get more of that scent. Then she stopped herself short and flung it on the floor.

Olivia, you fucking freak.

She got up and took the opportunity to change into pajamas, an old tank top and sleep shorts. She thought maybe getting out of that sweatshirt would chill her out, but nope.

The tension between the two of them was thick as California fog.

She got back into bed and she let her fingers breach the lacy waistband of her thong.

Chapter 4

OLIVIA CLOSED HER EYES, WILLING HERSELF TO THINK ABOUT anything or anyone that was even remotely attractive to her. Harry Styles. The bartender down the street who gave her free drinks. Her old neighbor...that one yoga instructor with the red hair and big tits...

But her mind kept wandering to the sound of the shower in the bathroom just a few feet away.

More memories. That time when she and Henry made out beneath the stadium at the homecoming game at her university. He was a year older than August, but was visiting from his much more elite undergrad. Henry and Olivia had been bickering all night, until Elliot pulled her aside and said, "So when you gonna fuck him, Liv?"

"What, me? We pretty much hate each other."

Elliot just shook her head. "You sweet, beautiful little creature."

And Elliot had been onto something because Olivia and Henry made out for two hours that evening. Her lips were red and chapped from his stubble. They didn't exchange numbers, and she fled before anyone found out.

The next morning, she'd been so upset to admit her

23

actions to August that she almost threw up in her Cheerios. But as would become a pattern, August brushed her off. "I do *not* want to know."

"As long as you're not mad."

"I'm not mad. You're an adult. He's an adult. But leave me so far out of it that I'm in Antarctica and you're in the Arctic."

"Those are two different things?" Olivia asked. August rolled her eyes. Elliot laughed.

The second time they hooked up was at a mutual friend's wedding. Olivia had been dancing all night with a tall, bearded man who apparently worked at something called a *hedge fund*. It was a decade ago, and at 23 she had no idea what a hedge fund was. She'd been an art history major for goodness sake. But as she was sauntering away to the bathroom, Henry appeared out of nowhere in his black and white tux, his dark hair a little mussed, his dark eyes as intense as ever. He sidled up right along next to her, his hands in his pocket, walking in step.

"Whatcha doing?" he asked.

She gave him an incredulous look. "This is a wedding, Henry. Maybe someday if you change your entire personality you'll get to experience one for yourself."

"Looks like you're flirting with that guy."

"What's it to you?"

Henry shrugged. "Nothing, except he's married." She later found out he was lying about that, but at twenty-three, she was aghast.

"Excuse me?"

"Yeah, and you're out there dancing...and grinding...with a married man..." he leaned in and whispered in her ear. "Very naughty."

She should've slapped the motherfucker, but she didn't. Instead, an intense thrill tightened in her belly. She'd never forgotten about their make out session behind the stadium.

She stopped abruptly, crossing her arms over her chest, which scooped up her cleavage in her strapless, black, sequined gown. Henry's eyes went dark, and he tugged at the corner of his collar with his long, elegant index finger. *Uh huh.* That's what she fucking thought. The alleged married hedge fund manager seemed all but a distant, passing thought when she had Henry so close.

"Follow me to the bathroom," she said.

Henry raised his brows, but then didn't ask another question, instead following lockstep right beside her. Then she dragged him into the bathroom stall and locked the door behind them. Their mouths collided in a kiss that was frantic and out of nowhere, but felt so right. She reached for the button on his pants, her hands eager for his cock, and he was already hard for her. That's how it was at twenty-four years old.

He breathed words into her ear as she pumped his dick. "That's right, right there, that's so hot. My cock's so fucking hard for you. God, you're so beautiful."

Afterwards, he'd tried to kiss her, letting his hands roam to the skirt of her ballgown, scrunching up the material to lift the hem, but she brushed him off. *Did she really just hook up with asshole Henry again? God, she was weak willed.*

"You don't want me to return the favor? Because I'd really like to," he said, his eyes glazed over from the orgasm. She opened up his suit jacket and rubbed the palm of her hand on the expensive inside liner, wiping his come along it.

"Nah, I've seen enough." And she reached behind him, opening the door and running away.

Had she been playing hard to get? No, she just knew better than to get too involved with Henry. She'd seen the kinds of women he dated before. They were all proto-types of Anna. Nothing like Olivia. Posh, pulled together women with their honey blonde hair tumbling down their backs in a single shining coil. At the time of the wedding, Olivia had just shaved half her head.

Henry was a square. He was a man destined to become a university graduation speaker some day. And as far as she could tell, he was an egomaniac. Not her type at all. She wouldn't get anything from him but a broken heart. He might look like a sensitive, brooding loner, but he was a heartbreaker.

And Olivia didn't get broken. She did the breaking.

The sound of the shower stopped, silence falling in its place. She heard the rake of the shower curtain. Then the echo of wet feet on the tile.

She pictured him now. Stepping out, naked, wet and hot. Water slicking down his long, muscled legs. His nearly black hair would be dripping and falling over his forehead. That's when she realized that her hand had been at work ....exploring the folds of her pussy, gently circling over her own clit, glimmers of sensation passing through her. She was wet too.

Dammit Olivia, you still managed to fantasize about Henry!

She jerked her hand out just in time for the door to burst open. Steam curled into the air from the opening of the doorway. And then it hit her.

The scent.

His scent. Not faint and wavering like the shirt he'd thrown at her. Strong now. Lingering. Wafting through the air. That same tangy, clean scent she remembered from all those years ago. Like fresh laundry, but better. It hadn't changed at all.

And the bastard knew what he was doing. She'd told him once when they'd gotten drunk after a last call at a bar near their condo building.

They'd ducked into an alley, her back against the brick wall, her hand in his thick hair, their tongues going wild, sloppy, because they were a little tipsy.

"Why are you doing this?" he whispered, pulling away from the magnetic kisses.

"I don't know you just smell so fucking good."

Olivia buried her head in her phone, pretending to be absolutely interested in what was on her screen as Henry walked by in nothing but a pair of grey sweatpants. No shirt at all. Just as she'd imagined, his pale skin was slightly red with warmth from the shower, and his hair was wet, flopping over one eyebrow.

He was hot enough to make a nun give up her vow of celibacy, but she could avoid all of that. His whole-entire, half-naked, damp frame, if only he just didn't *smell so good.*

She breathed in deep without even meaning to.

Immediately, he caught her eye as he stalked by the bed. She wanted to look away, but she couldn't.

He rounded the corner, and she *knew* she should look away, but she still couldn't.

Then he pulled up the sheet and slid his legs beneath the duvet.

"Should I turn off the lamp?" Olivia asked, in what she hoped was a disinterested tone.

"No, I'm not tired yet."

Her pussy basically throbbed at this point, which was annoying. She didn't even have to look at him. Aside from his full bodied intoxicating scent, she could just *sense* his presence. The heat radiating from his body. The heavy weight of him sinking into their shared mattress.

And then, for the next thirty minutes he proceeded to do the worst thing he'd ever done to her in the history of their interactions together.

He ignored her.

Like completely. Just sat there with his tablet, tapping away like she wasn't even fucking there.

What the fuck, Henry?

She fidgeted with her nails, clicking the tips back and forth before glancing at him furtively. He didn't move a goddamn centimeter.

She sighed loudly, turning on her side. Then she tapped on random things on her phone. Nothing was interesting. Everything was boring. She was too distracted now by the man in her bed.

She let out a fake laugh, pretending like she'd just read something funny.

No response. *Fine.*

Then, she scrolled on her phone, tutting her tongue and murmuring little *wows and damns.*

But nothing!

He wasn't going to take the bait, no matter what. And for some reason, at that very second, she absolutely couldn't stand it. She'd have to take drastic measures.

She flipped over so she was facing him. He was scrolling through what looked like a local news site, completely innocuous. She had an idea.

"Oh my god. Are you watching porn?" she asked in an over-exaggerated tone.

His tapping finger paused. He blinked slowly. "Excuse me? I'm reading the news."

She scooted a touch closer. "You are, aren't you? Don't lie to me. You're a pervert."

This time he narrowed his eyes, turning his head to look at her. "Are you insane?"

But she shuffled up to sit against the headboard. "Show me."

"Show you what?"

"The porn you're watching…"

He shook his head. "I'm not looking at porn. You're being weird, which is saying something."

But she persisted. "I bet it's absolutely dirty and disgusting. Just like you."

For a second longer, it seemed like he didn't get it, that she was attempting to provoke him. He looked ready to deny her accusations again, but then, he tilted his head, realization dawning. He tapped on his screen a few times. "You got me. I'm watching porn."

"I fucking knew it."

He raised an eyebrow. "You wanna see?"

Her belly did an excited little flip, but she scowled at him. "Don't be sick."

"Awww. But you seemed so interested just a moment ago. Here look..." he turned his screen to her. "I'll even let you pick a new one. Go on...whatever kink turns you on the most."

An actual porn site was pulled up on Henry's tablet now.

Welp, Olivia. He took the bait. What do you do now? You gonna reel him in?

She didn't know anything about reeling, but she did know how to ratchet. "I'm not picking anything because I'm not a fucking pervert like you. You probably love to watch a woman down on her knees choking on a man's enormous cock. Getting it all wet and sloppy....sliding her tongue up and down and up and down...You probably love that because you're such a disgusting pig."

"Blow jobs it is. Look, here's a Santa Claus themed one."

"You sick fuck."

"It is sick, isn't it...the way she's taking his cock like that. I wonder if you've ever taken a cock like that before? Right down your throat."

Olivia licked her lips, her gaze lingering over the video as it played. "Psh, please, I could do it so much better than that."

He raised his brows. "Really? She's a *professional.* In a Santa hat and everything."

Olivia pointed a finger at him. "How *dare* you suggest I wouldn't be as good as this woman at blowjobs. In fact, I think she could even do a better job than she's doing. Not to criticize, she's doing a very good job." She pointed at the paused screen. "But if it were me, I'd lean my head back a little more, for a better angle, so that his cock could hit right at the back of my throat, and then I'd guide his hand to the back of my head, let him fist my hair there, and hold my jaw so he could fuck my face. Sometimes it's better to work harder, not smarter. And also that way, when he comes, I'm ready to swallow it all the way down."

She gave him a smug look, but his eyes were squeezed shut, jaw tight.

"Hellooooo…" she crooned. "Earth to Henry…"

But he clicked off the screen and set the tablet on the nightstand to his left. "It's time to stop."

"What, you can't take a little grown-up talk? A little *friendly* discourse between two adults?"

He shook his head slowly. "You're unbelievable."

Olivia was confused. Maybe this was a little further than the usual barbs they threw back and forth, but it wasn't so far out of the realm. They hooked up, that's what they did. Henry was a grump. And Olivia couldn't read his goddamn mind!

Her phone dinged next to her, and she immediately turned on the screen. "Look, a match from one of my dating apps." She held it up to show to Henry. Maybe this would bring him back to his usual derision. Make fun of her for her poor choices in men or whatever it was he liked to do.

"This guy's profile says six foot three and enjoys stand up comedy."

"Yes, the cornerstone of all good personalities," Henry mumbled.

"He says he wants to meet. That he has extra Christmas presents if I'm interested. Wonder what he means by that…" she teased. She waited for his response, but nothing. "What? No snarky comment? Worried Santa is going to figure out you're a naughty boy."

"I'm sorry, am I having the same interaction as you or are we in two completely different worlds?"

Olivia scrunched her face. "Excuse me?"

"You were just watching *literal* Santa porn with me and describing the way you'd give a blowjob, and now you're about to entertain some douchebag who thinks he can meet up with you during a fucking blizzard. Is this normal?"

"Maybe he owns a snowplow."

"That's your takeaway from everything I just said?"

She shoved her hands in her hair, pulling it at the scalp. "Henry. It's me. Olivia."

"I know your name. And I know who you are."

"What's your problem?" Why was he being so...honest?

He looked at her, brows drawn, eyes incredulous, then he stumbled out of the bed. And before he could turn around, she saw it.

His absolutely bulging erection.

"Oh my god, *what* is that?" She knew she sounded imma-ture and a little mean, but maybe if she acted like a brat, he'd joke with her again. But instead, he froze and then slowly rotated to face her, the enormous bulge of his cock straining against his grey sweatpants.

Oh shit. That cock was no joke.

"I think you know exactly what this is..." He gestured toward his erection. "And I think you know exactly why I have it."

Oh how the turntables have turned... "I—I..." she searched for a quippy remark but she could find none. She hadn't actually *seen* Henry this way before. All their hookups had almost exclusively been furtive, drawn away, too dark or too smushed together to actually get an eyeful.

But it was bared to her now, his whole body displayed like that before her. His skin was pale, and although he wasn't very hairy, there was still something so manly about the way he stood. Confident but vulnerable. Veins running down his fore-arms, his fingers long and blunt, strong...with what she knew had surgeon dexterity. His legs were long, pulled apart, hips trim and narrow. The dim light highlighting the shadow of his abs.

Olivia had always been confident, her confidence had even grown over the years, harvested and tended to, along with her professional life where confidence was highly rewarded. Nobody wanted a hairdresser who was unsure of herself or her work.

But right now, even while her lust skyrocketed, her confidence wavered.

"Cat got your tongue?" Henry smirked. Then he tsk tsk tsked. He knew it. The power dynamic had shifted back in his favor. "Like what you see..." he stalked closer to the side of the bed, his shadow stretching before him. "Wanna see more?"

She swallowed hard, licked her lips without even thinking about it, when his fingers went to the waistband of his pants. He hooked his index and middle finger beneath the elastic— and her own fingertips could *feel* his taught skin there as he ran them along the horizontal band. Then, very slowly, he dragged the waistband ever so slightly lower, exposing the v-shaped indent flanking his lower abdomen. The skin pulled even tighter there, and the precipice of dark, trimmed pubic hair peeped through.

She sat up straighter. *Get yourself together, bitch. You aren't some fucking coward.* Plus, Henry had quite literally *never* looked hotter. Not behind the stadium at the football game with his youthful glow and not even at a friend's wedding when he was clean cut and pressed into a tuxedo.

Right there, right at that moment, was the hottest he—nay *anyone*—had ever appeared. Messy, wet, half-naked, sinewy, a little tired. Residency had aged him but had aged him into the man he was supposed to be.

Kind of like how Olivia had aged into her own body, her curves, her stretch marks, and the soft swell of her belly. She used to hate it, but now she loved it. She was grown.

They both were.

Or so she suspected as he stood in front of her half naked with a hard-on.

"Last chance..." he said, his voice nothing more than a whisper.

She inclined her chin. "Pull it down. Just...just a little."

His face was so dead serious, she could've sworn to god she'd never seen anyone look more serious. But his hands got to work. and he lowered the waistband enough to expose the ruddy, swollen head of his cock.

She almost fucking gasped. She bit her tongue to stop herself. "Move closer."

For one hot moment of insanity, she thought to herself, *put your mouth on it, let your tongue swirl around the head. Show him just how good you are at this.*

Her heart beat hard, and her clit was throbbing at the sight of him. So dark and brooding, but also clearly lusting after her. They always had lust. "Pull it down more..." she whispered and licked her lips.

He paused, but only for a moment, before stretching the waistband to reveal his long, thick shaft, a vein running down the length right to his balls. If someone had sent her a picture of this, she might not think it was hot, but in the moment, in the context of their situation, she needed a fucking fan.

"Well?" His voice was hoarse, and she realized she'd been staring. "Now that it's out, what do you want to do with it?"

Careful, Olivia. She leaned back. "Nothing." She gave him a serene smile.

And he let out a scoff, letting the waistband snap up around his hips again. "Games, games, games, Liv. All you do is play." He reached out to her face and he tucked a strand of hair behind her ear. She was taken aback by the gesture, his finger trailing along the line of her jaw before disappearing. But then, his voice changed abruptly, his arms going up in the air. "I tried to ignore you. But I'm stuck with you. In this *fucking* hotel."

Just like that awe slipped back into indignation. "Like I said, you could always sleep in the hallway."

He raked his hands over his wet hair. "Oh, I see, back to pretending again! Like nothing happened, literally seconds ago. Just jokes now. Ha ha."

"What has happened between us, Henry? You've never seemed to care before."

"What's that supposed to mean?"

Her cheeks heated. They always did the thing, they never named the thing. But now it suddenly seemed like Henry was ready to name all the things. The full stark reality of their interactions. But was she? "You know what it means."

"I know you don't need to use good words for your job, but try it now."

She glared at him. "You're an asshole."

Then he sat down on the bed next to her and sighed loudly. "I'm sorry, I didn't even mean that, I don't know why I said it."

"You said it because you're an egotistical prick." And that was exactly why she'd never admit her feelings.

He laughed a little at that. "You're not wrong." Then he exhaled. "Half the problem is our timing. One of us is always on and one of us is always off. No matter what."

"I think we have bigger problems than just that." *But no, that probably summed it up.* "I never said I was interested in you, anyway."

"No. No, of course not. You would never *say* anything like that. But actions speak louder than words."

She shrugged. "I'm a woman. I have needs. You live close by."

A pause stretched out between them before he spoke again. "I'm close by right now. How are your needs?" His voice was hoarse, he almost sounded resigned.

A shiver ran up her spine. "This time doesn't count."

"Why not?"

"I don't like you like that." A big fat, whopping lie. But one she wouldn't admit to even under the threat of physical harm.

"That's what you always say right before you jump my bones. Every fucking time."

"I've never jumped your bones. We've never even fucked before."

"Admit that you like me. C'mon, would it kill you?"

But the mention of Anna earlier had raised her hackles. She wouldn't give him the satisfaction. Maybe in the moment he was suddenly willing to talk frankly about their past liaisons, but what about tomorrow? Or the next day? Or when they returned to Charleston? What would happen then? "I've said it before, and I'll say it again, I don't even like you enough to want to share this bed with you."

He smirked. "Interesting because you liked me enough to jerk me off in the bathroom at that wedding ten years ago. You liked me enough to let me finger you on your couch four years ago. You liked me enough to make out with me on the rooftop of our building at sunrise seven weeks ago. And you liked me enough to text me an *accidental*," he added, using air quotes, "Picture of your ass in a glittery thong exactly....eigh-teen days ago."

There it was. Everything they'd done together...well, maybe not everything. But certainly some of the highlights. Rolled out like an ancient scroll. She brought her hand to her forehead. "What are you, like, keeping track of all our..." she cleared her throat. "Encounters."

"Yes." He answered without hesitation.

"Why?"

"Because I'm waiting for you to grow up."

Oh great, here he went again with his judgmental bullshit. He truly thought he was so much better than her. He and *Anna* were so perfectly fitted together. Why was she ever nice to him? She rolled her eyes. "*Fuck. You.*"

He opened his arms wide. "I'm ready whenever you are, baby."

"Agh!" She couldn't believe that for even a second she'd let herself think that *maybe* he actually had real feelings for her. No, it was about getting the upper hand. Well, she wouldn't let him have it. "Fine, if you want to put it all out in the open then that's fine with me. You want the dirty honest truth about us, Henry?"

"Yes actually, I would like that, but I don't think you're capable."

"Sometimes when I think about you my skin itches like the fucking plague. Sometimes I just want to forget that I know you, like I wish I could cut out the part of my brain that remembers any second we've spent together. Sometimes when you're in the same room as me I have the urge to run. I always give you another chance to be a friend and you *always* act like a colossal dick instead." Like why didn't he ever call her after their hookups? Why did she always have to find out through the grapevine weeks later that he was back with Anna? "You're nothing but a self-centered twat who cuts people's hearts out all day." And her heart wouldn't be one of them. She narrowed her eyes. "Quite frankly you enrage me. You make me want to scream." She hustled out of the bed, flinging the comforter off and marching to the bathroom.She could hear him right behind her.

"Oh, I *enrage* you? Me, who saves lives all day? What do you do for people? Overpriced blowouts?"

She stopped abruptly. She might not be a heart surgeon, but she did make people's lives better. She spun around. "My blowouts aren't overpriced. They're priced exactly right. People will pay a lot of money to get blown out by me!" Then she jabbed him in the sternum with one long, manicured nail. "You included."

"Oh please. I don't have to pay you for that."

"You're still obsessed with that handjob I gave you after all these years. Well, newsflash: I was on Molly! I would've jerked off the goddamn bartender, but he rejected me earlier that night. That's what you do when you go to a wedding with Elliot Sheer. You take Molly. Until your little show just now, I didn't even remember what your dick looked like. I didn't even remember what it felt like. I didn't even remember how big it was. *That's* how memorable you are to me." *A big lie, she remembered it all.*

He took a step closer, but she refused to acquiesce her space. "You might fool everyone else with this fun-time-princess persona, but you don't fool me, Liv. I know you remember." He leaned down, his teeth against the fold of her ear. "Just like me."

She squeezed her thighs together but then stepped forward, shoulder checking Henry out of the way. "One thing you shouldn't forget about me, Henry…is that I'm just as good with sharp objects as you are." *I'll cut your heart out too, mother-fucker, just try me.*

'I'm asking for real, Liv. Do you want this or not? For real. Do you want me?"

She stopped and faced him again, hands on her hips. She was too wound up to answer or to even process what he was asking. "How many times did you break up with Anna, only to get back together again? How many times did you come knocking on my door late at night when you two were on one of your *breaks?* I'm not your fallback plan until you marry Anna."

"I'm not marrying Anna."

"That's a lie. Call Maury. Get the polygraph."

He shook his head. "You can't even answer a fucking question. Every time I think I'm getting anywhere with you, you just put up more walls. You act like nothing's transpired at all between us. We play this fucking game of pretend.

37

You act like I don't even exist after we hook up. And you know what?" He threw his hands up. "I deserve this. I let you use me. I take your scraps like a goddamn puppy. We pretend to be friends. We pretend to be enemies. It grows old."

Holy shit, what was he even saying? He acted like *she* didn't exist! Had they both been ignoring each other? "Scraps? Excuse me?" She was the one always taking scraps.

"You even invited me on this trip, and like a fool I said yes. And don't act like it was some matter of convenience. You wanted me to come. You wanted some excuse to torture me a little bit after an evening of too much drinking. To tempt me into touching you, sneaking around late at night like we always do."

"We only do all that sneaking around because I'm the person you secretly fuck around with in the off season. After all this, you're going to go back to Anna anyway. Just like you've done a million times before. That's why I avoid you after we hook up. And it's not like you come seek me out afterward either."

He rubbed his palms down his face. "I don't seek you out because immediately after we hook up you act like you've committed a federal fucking crime! It's not exactly encouraging. In fact, quite the opposite." Henry let out an exasperated sound. One she'd never heard from him, one that came from his chest. It was a little sad and a little angry all at once. He collapsed on the end of the bed. "Anna broke up with me this time."

"So?"

"She's never done that before. Usually, it's me who ends things, and then she convinces me to come back later, and I do because...well, because she takes my mind off...stuff. And it was easy. Predictable. But it's over forever now. She said something that neither of us could ever unhear."

Olivia's face was frozen in a questioning stare. "What did

she say?" She could barely find her words, but her curiosity overcame her pride.

Beats of silence skipped on before he answered. "She said she couldn't be with me when it was so obvious..." he stabbed his hand through his hair, frustrated. "It was so obvious that I was in love with someone else."

Olivia's eyes went wide, her stomach feeling like it was slipping on ice. "Why would you be in love with someone else?"

"I don't know, Liv. You tell me."

She shook her head. He couldn't be saying what she thought he was saying. There was no fucking way. "I don't believe you."

"I knew you wouldn't."

Her heart began pounding in her chest, her vision a little blurry. "If it's true, then say it." She crossed her arms. "Say it outloud. I dare you."

He stalked closer to her, his gaze dark, the glint in his eye hard and steely. She couldn't look away, even when he tilted his head with a glare. "I. Fucking. *Hate*. You." His voice broke with the words.

But she knew that *hate* wasn't the word he really meant to say.

She was torn between crying and yelling, but instead...out of nowhere, a laugh expelled from her chest. "Well, I fucking hate you, too. From the moment I laid eyes on you. From the very second we met. I've never hated anyone more." She chuckled, rubbing her eyes. What in the actual fuck was happening? Was this real life?

Then he laughed too and an uncharacteristically sheepish look crossed his face. He scratched his head. "You mean it?"

Her head fell back. "Fuck, I really do. I hate you so much."

"Good." He reached out, his hand grabbing hers. "C'mere." With gentle effort, he drew her near, until she was right against his chest, engulfed in his clean scent, her chin tipped back. And just like that, the atmosphere between them flipped.

"I'm still mad at you," she murmured.

"I like it when you're a little mad..." His hand found its way to the hair at the base of her neck.

"You would." Although, she liked when he was all geared up too. Her vision went a little droopy as he stroked her hair.

And he bent his head over her, her heart racing as their lips meant in the softest of kisses. More delicate and soft than any kiss they'd ever shared before. She raised up on her tippy toes to get even closer to him, her hands threading into the silky dark hair at his neck. And just like that, the kiss gained heat and speed. His hand pressed down the front of her body, groping her breast, pinching her nipple and then squeezing lightly again.

He wasn't gentle, but he knew what he was doing. Her body might as well have burst into flames.

"Turn around."

Her eyes shot open. "What?"

"I said turn the fuck around." His hand then drifted from her hair down her back, fingers flexing against her skin, goose-bumps rippling up her shoulders.

"Why?"

"Because I'm still mad at you too. And we're gonna learn a lesson. Together."

Chapter 5

Olivia stared at Henry good and hard, and then squeezed her eyes shut and pivoted slowly on the balls of her feet.

"Good girl. Now, up against the wall."

"Excuse me?" she squeaked. She didn't know this side of Henry. Their other hookups were messy but always with an air of levity, but this time he seemed serious. Why did that especially appeal to her?

But his voice was steady. "You heard me. Put your hands up against the wall. Go on."

Gingerly, she cleared her throat. *Okay then!* And rested her hands against the smooth drywall. Inwardly, she ached with anticipation and vibrated with excitement. Whatever was happening between her and Henry was different than it'd ever been. What remained the same was that she was too weak to say no to it. She could never say no to him.

She shivered when his hand moved her hair to one side of her shoulder fingertips gliding along, exposing the vulnerable skin of her neck. But then she yelped when he yanked her by the hips, her ass pushed against his pelvis, his cock hard and unyielding behind her.

Moisture rushed between her thighs and heat flushed over her sternum when his breath was at her ear. "You can't act like this never happened..." he whispered.

She didn't move a fucking muscle, but that wasn't good enough for him. "I'm gonna need an answer from you, Liv."

"What's the...what's the question?" She licked her lips, shocked by the desperate breathy tone of her own voice. She wanted to buck her hips back into him.

"I'll put my cock inside you so deep and fuck you so good I'll have you singing Christmas carols for a year. But I won't do it unless you promise you won't pretend afterwards."

She nodded, her forehead pushed against the wall. "Yeah...yeah..."

"Yeah what?"

"I promise."

"Be specific. Use my name."

"I promise I won't pretend, Henry. I want it."

"Where do you want it, Liv?"

Oh shit. It was like he wanted a covenant between them. An oath.

But so did she. "Deep inside me...please...do it now..."

One hand pulled down her sleep shorts, letting them fall to her ankles, while his other hand ran down the curve of her ass, fingers hooking into the string of her thong, yanking it down her thighs. Her ears perked at the snap of his waistband, and she could feel the motion behind her of him pulling off his pants. When she caught the sight of his grey pants hitting the floor, she had to swallow hard. Henry Pointe was standing behind her totally and completely naked.

The head of his dick nudged beneath her legs. "Wider..." he commanded, prompting her to spread her legs apart so he could fist his cock and rub it against the delicate skin between her thighs. "You're so fucking wet," he murmured.

She knew she was. She could feel him spreading the moisture around her pussy with his cock, the circular gliding sensation of the velvety, hot skin against hers making her knees tremble with desire. "Please, just do it…"

"Pushy, pushy…" He tsked, but she gasped when at the same time he pushed into her, the slow penetration taking her breath away.

He rocked without hurry, pushing in past the head. And she bucked against him to take him in deeper until he was all the way to the hilt.

"Fuck…" he groaned. Her pussy twitched around his thick cock as he penetrated her deeply, all while the feelings within her sweltered. She'd never been so close to Henry before, the very concept stole her breath away. But she had no time to contemplate her feelings because Henry began to move.

His hips rolled into her earnestly at first, a staccato groan with each thrust, and sparks of pleasure shot into her lower belly. Then he fisted her hair, pulling her head back from the wall, his lips against her ear.

"Tell me you like it when I fuck you. Tell me I'm the only one…that you feel it too." He was fucking her hard now, her body jolting against the wall. "Go on."

"I feel it too…" she could barely get the words out, the feeling of his body pressed against hers, the swell of his cock inside her pussy, the sound of their bodies colliding again and again and again.

"And we aren't pretending like this never happened," he said, his tongue flicking out along her ear.

She tried to shake her head, but he was pounding into her so hard now she could feel it in the back of her throat. "No…no…"

"Because you can't forget me, Liv…Just like I can't forget you…" His hand snaked around her waist then traveled up to grab her breast. "God, I love your fucking body."

"I wish I could see yours," she spit out, rocking her hips back to meet his thrusts, her lungs working overtime now.

"You will. Are you close?"

"Almost."

"Touch yourself. Now."

Oh fuck, she reached between her body and the wall and began rubbing flat handed and sloppily against her clit. Henry's hands held onto both of her breasts, his long fingers gently squeezing each nipple. "When you come I want you to say my name, prove that this happened."

"Mmm....mmmm," she mewled in response. Although her cheek was pressed against the side of the wall, Henry leaned against her, licking into her mouth, an almost kiss but it was too messy and dirty. Another moan came out of her, and seeing that it was working, he did it again, licking her lips.

She swallowed as her body collected all the experiences around her. His lips, now pressed against her neck pushing hot breath against her own perspiration, her hand rubbing her own clit at his command, his cock slapping into her, pushing her into the wall so that she was anchored to reality, locked in place with nothing but him tethering her in space and time.

"I can tell you're... going to... come," he panted, his words rough. "I know you."

Even while fucking he was completely full of himself. She was full of him too, though. She almost giggled at the thought, but an acute sensation caught in her throat instead and burst through the rest of her body.

Then, the culmination of it all, hit her hard and at once. "Fuckfuckfuckfuckfuck, Henry, yes..." she practically hiccuped as the orgasm ripped through her.

His pace steadied, and even as her own hand fell from her clit, she could still feel the reverberations of pleasure pulsing through her with each penetration. He grabbed her hand in his and held it against her pussy.

"God, I love hearing my name while you come around my cock..." Then he pushed into her limp body a few more times. He wrapped his arms around her so tightly she thought she might pass out, but his body tensed and then slackened, finally out of breath as he came inside of her.

He rested his cheek against her back. "I can't believe we just did that." His words were followed with an uncharacteristic little chuckle.

She found herself laughing absently as well. She was still lost to the sensations of the moment, his hot body pressed against her, his come dribbling down her inner thigh, the post orgasm buzz vibrating softly through her entire being.

Gently, he pulled out of her, and her breath caught at the loss of him. Then he turned her around to face him. And he pulled her in for a kiss, his fingers threading through her hair, his palms cupping her jaw. Urgent but sweet. When he released her, a new kind of look glinted in his eyes. Something flickering deeply behind them. She couldn't name it, but she could feel it.

"Henry?"

He pulled on his pants and kneeled down to lift up her underwear and shorts around her thighs. "Yeah?"

"Can we lie on the bed? Together?" This time was different from the other times. Every other time they'd messed around, they would part ways afterwards, coldness growing between them with each interaction.

But now, she was just heating up. And she needed something. Something she couldn't quite identify.

A hug?

Her feelings rubbed raw in her heart and throbbed painfully when Henry took her hand in his and pulled her down next to him on the bed.

"Tuck your legs under…" he said as he lifted up the tightly fitted duvet. She slid beneath the blanket and scooted in next to him. But he pulled her in even closer, wrapping his arm around her shoulder and leaving her no choice but to rest her head on his chest. Her eyelids fluttered at the steady, rhythmic beat of his heart. Soothing in a way she'd never expected. Warmed up like a heated blanket.

"So, how're we gonna ensure we don't fall back into bad habits?" she mused in her half hypnotized state.

"Well, even though I've already confessed that I...hate you. I think we should consider taking things slow."

"Sure, but we should still have sex, right?"

"Oh for sure, we should definitely keep having sex."

She laughed. "But I hear what you're saying. We need to talk. Openly. Honestly."

He patted her shoulder. "Yes, exactly."

A pang of nervousness sparked in her belly. "But you first. Just so I can make sure you do it right."

"Okay. Here goes. It's always been you, Liv. I've never met anyone like you. Friendly, confident, artistic. And you never try to be like anyone else. I love that about you. I always have. I always will. You're the person who I always wanna be around. I even moved into your fucking building, for godsake."

She giggled. "You said it was because my building was so close to the hospital!"

"An obvious and transparent lie."

"Wow." She swallowed hard. For some reason, she hadn't expected all that, but now that he'd said it, she realized that she'd always known it too. Her turn, then. "Okay, cards on the table. I used to go to the bar by our building all the time in the hopes that I'd run into you."

His arms squeezed around her shoulder. "I knew it!"

"*And* I'd even bring my dates there just to make you jealous."

"It worked. Too well sometimes. I was mostly convinced you hated me. Like for real, hated me."

"I mean, I did. Especially when you were always with Anna."

"Well. That should've been over long ago."

"It's okay. It's not like I ever told you any of this before. Or like you ever told me."

"God, what were we thinking? We could've been together this whole time."

Her hand trailed over his chest to catch his hand, interlacing their fingers. "Merry Christmas, Henry."

He kissed her forehead. "Merry Christmas, Liv."

"So, what happens next?" She breathed in deep, the clean, tangy scent filling her with happiness.

"How about a date?"

"A real date? Not a frantic late night text message?"

"Nope, a real date. I'll pick you up."

She made a face. "How about I pick you up?"

"The Nissan is sturdy! I'll pick you up, I'll take you out somewhere nice. We'll have a real dinner. Sushi, your favorite."

"How'd you know that?"

He shrugged. You told that hedge fund manager that you loved spicy eel."

She lifted her head. "That was years ago."

Henry smiled slyly and tapped her wrist with each word. "I. Pay. Attention."

"To me?"

"To you. To everything you do."

"You lied to me that night and told me that guy was married."

"Yes, exactly! You're welcome."

She laughed but then a seriousness settled over her. "We can't tell August right away. Not until at least date three."

"Fine, you can tell her whenever you want, but I promise you one thing."

"What's that?"

"I'll be sneaking into your room at night if we ever make it to the mountain house."

She smiled. "I'd be devastated if you didn't."

"I've only ever wanted one person. I can't believe you didn't notice. I've only been chasing you for a full fucking decade."

She relaxed her tense muscles allowing herself to rest against his chest again. *Thump-thump, thump-thump, thump-thump.* "But all we do is bicker."

Henry shrugged. "I'm a Pointe. It's in our nature. It's how we show affection."

Olivia let out a soft laugh. It was true. His sister August wasn't the warmest of the bunch either. "But still…"

He squeezed her tightly. "And one more thing…"

"Hmm?" she hummed, her eyes getting droopy, the heat of his chest and the steady thump of his heart lulling her into a hot, peaceful daze.

"I wanna fuck you again in the morning. But I'm taking my time. Foreplay. Clothes off. Your body. My tongue. Everywhere."

She shivered. "Are you trying to say there wasn't any foreplay tonight? Because I beg to differ. I think we had several hours of foreplay. Fighting has always been our foreplay, hasn't it?"

And the chuckle from his chest reverberated into her ear. "Don't tempt me with a good time."

Chapter 6

OLIVIA WOKE UP SO HOT SHE THOUGHT SHE MIGHT BE ON FIRE. Henry's snores echoed in her ear. He snored. How whimsical for such a grouch. Her leg was slung over his bony hip, and his hand was tangled in her hair. Warmth spread from their enmeshed bodies. Sweat collected in her cleavage and between the press of his skin and hers. In a rush, every second from the night before came tumbling back into her consciousness sending a burst of excitement through her limbs.

At first she let out an audible gasp, her hand slapping over her mouth to cover the sound. And then before she could stop herself, giggles came pouring out of her. She had fucked Henry. She, Olivia Couper, had fucked him, Henry Pointe. Holy shit! And they didn't have to pretend like nothing happened afterwards. And double holy shit, based on the erection pushing against her leg, he probably wasnt lying when he said he wanted to fuck her again that morning.

"Hey…" he murmured, stretching his long arms out above her, stifling a yawn.

"Hey…" she murmured back. And then she turned her head and stared at him.

"What?" he laughed. "Why are you staring at me like that?"

Oh god. What have I done? Maybe he didn't mean any of it? She squeezed her eyes shut.

"Wait! Don't look away now!" Henry gathered her up in his arms, pulling her on top of his chest. "I had this wild dream that I confessed to you that I was in love with you and then fucked you from behind against a wall. And I have to verify with you that it was just a dream."

Heat crept into her cheeks. "Whoa. Crazy."

"It was some of the best dream sex of my life."

"Really? That's a high bar."

"But you know what I think now that I'm awake?"

"What's that?"

"I think we can do better…" He reached up and pulled her down so her lips met his.

Her hand covered his mouth right in the nick of time. "But let's brush our teeth first."

HENRY'S MINTY fresh tongue traveled the length from Olivia's belly button to her pelvis where he paused and glanced up. "Your pubic hair is hot pink."

"Yep."

"Have you always dyed it?"

"Maybe for the last five or six years…" But her voice was interrupted in a gasp as Henry's tongue touched the very tip of her clit. "Hoooooomygod…."

"I can't believe I didn't know this about you," Henry said before giving another lick. And then another. And another.

Olivia's voice shook. "Uhhhhuhhh…"

"I wanna know everything about you." He lapped at her again, this time maintaining a soft but steady, circular rhythm.

"Okay…yes…yes…" Olivia chanted, her hands coming to

grasp onto his hair so she could direct him. Her hips rolled shamelessly against his tongue. "I'd fucking sell you the nuclear codes if you keep doing that…"

That spurred him on more, and he went after her with enthusiasm, a finger making its way into the mix, slowly penetrating her and then curling once deep inside.

She almost lost her shit, her eyes rolling in her head. "Fuck, Henry…right there…"

He followed instructions well. For once. Continuing to lick her center in conjunction with the come hither movement of his finger. She'd never felt anything like it. Maybe a medical degree really did teach him a thing or two about the human body. After all, he'd certainly been set on stealing her heart with tricks like that.

She got up on her elbows to watch him. She loved to see his face buried between her thighs, her fingers threaded into his thick dark hair. Her thighs were trembling, her orgasm building.

But then she saw his hand creep below his waist, his fist moving up and down. She realized he was jerking himself off while he went down on her.

"Mmm, yes, that's so fucking hot," she moaned, her hips moving in little short motions, his tongue swirling against her.

She heard him groan and felt the vibrations between her thighs, the stubble on his jaw scratching the sensitive skin. Henry Pointe was eating her pussy like it was the most expensive thing on the menu. And just like that, an orgasm bubbled up and through her.

"I'm coming, I'm coming….don't stop…" she eeked out, bucking her hips and tensing her legs so hard she was worried she would squish his head. But he was unphased by the squishing and he listened until every last drop of pleasure was wrung out of her body. She had to slap his face and hand away from her pussy. "I can't take anymore," she pleaded.

He nipped at the soft flesh at the inside of her thigh and

then rose up above her, hair a mess, eyes dark, lips swollen. He pulled down the collar of her already low cut tank top until each of her breasts were exposed and caged within the shirt. She yelped when he gave the shirt one more yank. His lips lowered over one hard nipple, the sensation running through her slack body like a livewire. Maybe she couldn't have another orgasm, but damn was Henry trying his luck.

"Your body is unbelievable…" he said on an inhale, and his mouth went for the other nipple, swirling over the hard tip until she let out a moan and then he ever so gently tugged on it between his teeth before letting go. His lashes, dark and thick. His hard dick tapped at the space between her legs.

Her libido was rebuilding with unparalleled speed.

Both his hands cupped her breasts so they squished together, creating a long valley of cleavage. "God, that's so hot." He leaned forward and licked a line from nipple to nipple. "I'm going to hold them together. You touch your-self….while I fuck your tits."

Olivia lifted her head. "Are you serious?"

He froze, arms tensed. "I mean, unless you don't want that."

Her lips parted, her head nodding. "Oh, I want that. I definitely want that." It sounded dirty. And hot. And with Henry? Sign her up.

She did as she was told, her hand reaching towards her clit, while Henry's hips settled above her, straddling her body. He fed the shaft in between her cleavage, large hands holding onto her, hips moving. She'd never done this before, but she loved a novel experience.

The velvety skin of his cock rubbed hard and hot against her own soft skin, the head peeking out between the valley of her breasts as he thrust. She watched it as her hand circled her clit, willing another orgasm even when she thought she was spent.

"Keep touching yourself…" Henry groaned as he worked

himself against her. His strained words spurred her on. His eyes were half glazed, half closed, the look on his face like he was off somewhere in space.

His thrusts gained momentum, and her hand did as well until they were both panting and the bed was squeaking with their frantic motions.

"I'm gonna come..." he huffed. "Are you going to come?"

She swallowed hard and nodded, her hand working fast. "You first..."

Her chin tilted back in concentration. His thrusts grew erratic and his hands groped at her until finally hot ropes of come slashed across her sternum. He stilled, panting.

He collapsed to her side, his mouth buried in the hair by her shoulder. "I guess I need to take over the job..." he said into her ear, and then pushed her hand away, his fingers taking its place.

She recognized the change in sensation immediately, his touch providing the right pressure but a new tempo against her skin, stirring the feelings around in her belly that she was trying so hard to coax out. He circled her clit, applying slightly more pressure and picking up speed, until her hips worked against him.

"So close..." she spit out, the muscles in her neck and jaw strained.

And then, he lifted his hand and gave her a tiny slap right over her clit. Her lips parted in a sharp intake, her body jerked, and when his fingers resumed their work an orgasm seeped down her like sap from a tapped Maple tree.

"Good girl, good girl..." he murmured as her body seized.

She let the orgasm roll through her, as deep whining moans escaped. Her vision blackened for one heightened moment, and then slowly she descended back into a soft wave on the mattress.

"Okay...okay. I'm done. No more." Her head lolled to the side of the pillow and her body was slack once again. His hand slowed to a stop and then disappeared. He nuzzled against her shoulder, kissing the outside shell of her ear.

She wasn't sure if she was dead or alive.

She leaned up on her elbows, surveying the mess he'd left on her skin, and dipped her fingertip into one of the white ropes, bringing it to her lips, licking off the salty come. His eyes went dark and he grabbed her hand, putting her fingers in his mouth as well, his tongue swirling around before he pulled them out.

"I will definitely never forget this," she breathed.

"Good."

He got out of the bed, and she watched him walk stark naked to the bathroom, returning with a wet washcloth. "Lean back..." he instructed, and he leaned over her wiping his come from her chest with easy motion.

She was touched by the way he was taking care of her. He set the towel on the nightstand and sprawled out beside her, his back against the headboard, hands rested in his lap. Both of them naked.

"How have we wasted so much goddamn time?" He asked, his words thoughtful. "I wanna spend every goddamn day of my life with you, Liv. If you'll have me. I don't want to wait another ten years."

She reached out, slipping her hand into his, bringing the shared clasp to her lips and kissing the back. "We didn't fuck slowly this time..." she mused.

He looked at her and smiled. "We'll just have to keep trying."

HENRY AND OLIVIA lay on the bed together, wrapped in towels, squeaky clean after a shower. The weather channel droned on from the TV on the wall across from them, but Olivia was barely conscious. Her body, her brain, her soul weren't even trying to do the math on the equation of circumstances that had befallen her within the last day and a half.

She didn't believe in miracles…but was this…what had happened…what was happening, between her and Henry…a motherfucking Christmas miracle?

She could almost laugh.

"Roads now open on twenty six headed west bound…" The words cut through her haze. She tapped Henry on his bare chest. "Hey…hey…you hear that?"

"Hmm?" he asked, his gaze staring down her cleavage, his knuckles grazing over her left nipple.

"The roads are cleared. We can go! We can make it to the mountains." Quickly she reached for her phone on the nightstand. Elliot had already texted from the airport.

Elliot: Bitch, I got a flight! I'll be there tonight in t-minus-four-hours.

Olivia smiled and tapped out a message as well.

Olivia: Roads are plowed! Everything's open. See you soon!

Chapter 7

OLIVIA SUCKED ON A SMALL CANDY CANE IN THE PASSENGER seat of Henry's car as he efficiently packed their luggage into the trunk. When he finished, he opened the driver door, bent his tall body inside, and gave her a serious look.

"Whaaa?" she asked, mouth full of candy cane.

He shook his head. "Nothing. I love you."

Her cheeks went hot. "I love you, too…" She spit out, but the words were muffled.

He smiled, reached over and drew the small candy cane from her mouth, popping it into his own, the end sticking out like a Christmasy cigarette. Then he tossed something onto her lap.

"What do you want me to do with this?" She handled the small Christmas gift that she'd thrown into the back seat at the beginning of their trip.

"It's for you."

She smirked. "You said it was from a patient."

He crunched on the candy cane and shrugged. "I lied. Open it."

Gingerly she slipped her nail beneath the seam of the red and white wrapping, peeling off the festive paper and unveiling a plain, rectangular box. "This is so weird..." she murmured.

"Keep going."

She pulled off the lid revealing a pair of shiny, cobalt alloy scissors with a cat's eye blade resting on top of crushed black velvet. She weighed the cold metal in her hand. "Henry, these scissors cost hundreds of dollars."

"Like you said, you're just as good with sharp objects as I am. A blade fit for a princess." And he winked at her, turning the ignition, his old ass Nissan Sentra fighting for its life, but roaring awake. Her heart melted like icicles in her chest.

"I don't even know what to say."

He ran his hand through his thick, dark hair. "Maybe you could cut my hair sometime."

She let out a laugh. "I've literally been dying to do so!"

The rest of their drive was smooth and quiet, plowed highways and banked snow. The outside air lingered still and cold, but the inside air between them had warmed toasty and light.

And Olivia grabbed Henry's thigh when the enormous mountain house came into view with its huge, metallic ornaments hanging from the overgrown, front-yard trees to the dangling icicle lights covering every shingle of the roof.

Snow blanketed the earth surrounding them.

"Wow..." she whispered.

He nodded. "It's pretty magical, huh?"

They rolled up on the long, gravel driveway. She tripped out of the car excitedly, and he joined on the walk up the path, hands in the pockets of his jeans.

Then, they approached the entrance, side by side.

He looked over at her. "We made it."

"Against all odds."

And Olivia opened the door.

Acknowledgments

Thank you to all the great people in my writing community who've helped me get this far: SJ Tilly, G.Marie, S.L. Astor, Elaine Reed, Love Mikayla Eve, and many, many more.

And thank you to my cover designer Beatrix Sawad who went the extra mile making sure I actually had a cover for this book.

Special shout out as always to my partner for constantly going out of his way to support me.

And lastly, thanks to my dogs who always keep me company even in the darkest of nights.

Happy Holidays.

About the Author

Cat Wynn lives in a cozy house in Charleston, SC with her long-time partner and two geriatric rescue dogs. She writes late at night on an old couch that should've probably been thrown out five years ago. She's a shockingly good time at parties provided the snacks are good. You can test this theory by inviting her to your wedding.

You can find Cat on most platforms @catwynnauthor. You can also listen to her wax philosophical about romance novels and writing on her podcast Tall, Dark & Fictional. And if you want to know even more about her you can visit her website, www.catwynnauthor.com and subscribe to her newsletter at https://catwynnauthor.substack.com/

Also by Cat Wynn

Partner Track

Perdie Stone needs just three things in life: Her forever best friend, Lucille. Their adorable rescue pug, Bananas. And last but not least, a coveted partnership at her Charleston law firm.

A partnership she more than deserves when she goes head-to-head with hotshot Ivy League attorney Carter Leplan on a big case and comes out on top. She didn't think anything would feel better than beating the annoyingly gorgeous lawyer at his own game, but that's before a freak storm leaves them both stranded.

Together.

In the last hotel room.

With only one bed.

It's a one-night stand Perdie isn't soon to forget...especially after Carter turns up at her firm and slides right into the job that should have been hers. And right back into her life—a life she thought she had all figured out.

Holiday Games

After the worst year ever, August Pointe can't wait to spend Friendsmas with her besties at her uncle's mountain house. She could really use the comfort of a few familiar faces. But when a blizzard hits, August ends up stuck at the house with a mutual acquaintance she's never met instead.

But Jack Harris is a hot, TikTok famous chef. And something about his easy going nature and excellent drink making skills are thawing out August's icy exterior. Plus, he's brought a kitten with him!

August is reluctant to get involved, but some Christmas presents are too tempting to keep wrapped up. And her friends think she deserves a little holiday cheer. Still, August isn't sure if it's worth playing bedroom games with a stranger or if she'll just end up doubly heart broken by New Years.

Hotel Games

Hair stylist Olivia Couper can't wait to celebrate Friendsmas with her besties in a secluded mountain house. So, when Olivia asks Henry, her best friend's grumpy surgeon brother, to carpool, she swears it's a matter of convenience and not a bid for Henry's attention.

Sure, they've been hooking up for years, but they always followed one unspoken rule: Never talk about the hook ups.

Unfortunately, a blizzard hits while Olivia and Henry are on the road, stranding them in the last hotel room available. And suddenly, Henry wants to break all the rules.

Olivia's left with a choice: confront her real feelings for Henry or flee to the mountain house with all her walls intact. It's a game she isn't sure she's ready to play and a hotel stay she isn't soon to forget.

Made in United States
Orlando, FL
29 November 2022

25210217R00046